W9-CCL-622

DETROIT PUBLIC LIBRARY

LINCOLN BRANCH
1221 E. Seven Mile
Detroit, MI 48203

DATE DUE

FEB 1 3 1993
APR 1 5 1993

ROOTER REMEMBERS

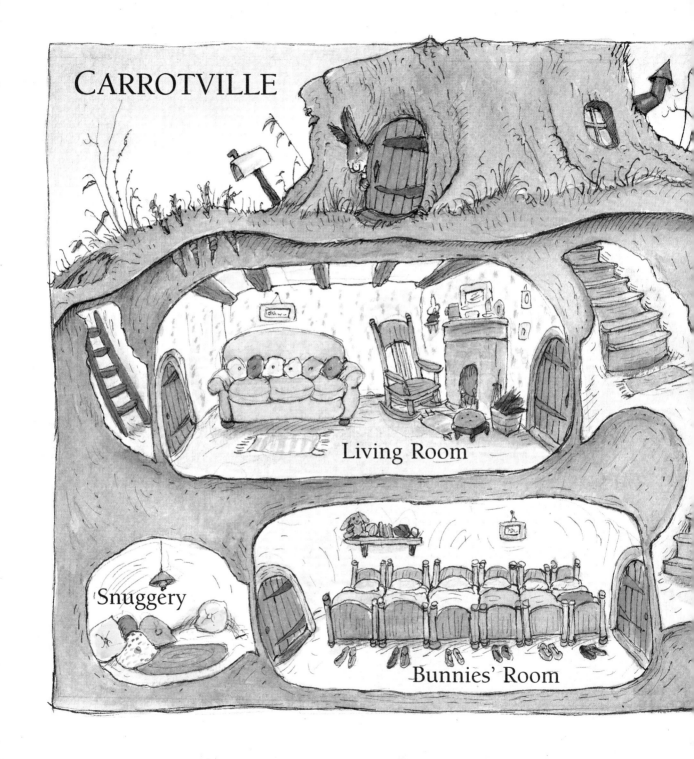

CARROTVILLE

Living Room

Snuggery

Bunnies' Room

Attic

Dining Room

Kitchen

Mama's
Room

Rhoda   Ricky Mama Margaret Rowdy Rooter Rena
Rabbit   Rose

ROOTER REMEMBERS

A BANK STREET BOOK ABOUT VALUES

by Joanne Oppenheim

Illustrated by Lynn Munsinger

VIKING

je cl

VIKING
Published by the Penguin Group
Viking Penguin, a division of Penguin Books USA Inc.,
375 Hudson Street, New York, New York 10014, U.S.A.
Penguin Books Ltd, 27 Wrights Lane, London W8 5TZ, England
Penguin Books Australia Ltd, Ringwood, Victoria, Australia
Penguin Books Canada Ltd, 2801 John Street, Markham, Ontario, Canada L3R 1B4
Penguin Books (N.Z.) Ltd, 182–190 Wairau Road, Auckland 10, New Zealand

Penguin Books Ltd, Registered Offices: Harmondsworth, Middlesex, England

First published in 1991 by Viking Penguin, a division of Penguin Books USA Inc.

1 3 5 7 9 10 8 6 4 2

Series graphic design by Alex Jay/Studio J
Editor: Gillian Bucky
Special thanks to James A. Levine, William H. Hooks, and Regina Hayes

Copyright © Byron Preiss Visual Publications, Inc., 1991

Text copyright © The Bank Street College of Education, 1991.

Illustrations copyright © Byron Preiss Visual Publications, Inc., and Lynn Munsinger, 1991.

All rights reserved

A Byron Preiss Book

Carrotville is a trademark of The Bank Street College of Education.

Library of Congress card catalog number: 00-00000

ISBN: 0-670-82865-3

Printed in Singapore

Without limiting the rights under copyright reserved above, no part of this
publication may be reproduced, stored in or introduced into a retrieval
system, or transmitted, in any form or by any means (electronic, mechanical,
photocopying, recording or otherwise), without the prior written permission
of both the copyright owner and the above publisher of this book.

To my grandson, Adam. Welcome!—J.O.
For Dan—L.M.

"One, two, three, four, five." Mama Rabbit counted the carrot pot pies she had baked for the picnic.

"That's strange," she said, "I baked six pies, one for each of my bunnies. I left them here to cool. But now one is gone."

"Rooter took it!"
said Rhoda.
"Did not,"
Rooter mumbled.

"He's lying!"
shouted Rowdy.
"Am not,"
Rooter grumbled.

"I saw him eat it," said Rena.

"Me, too," Ricky agreed.

"Tell the truth, Rooter," said Margaret Rose.

"You're all picking
on me!" cried Rooter.

"Children, please, let's give Rooter a chance."
Mama Rabbit looked at Rooter. "All right, Rooter,
tell the truth. Did you take a carrot pot pie?"

"No, Mama," said Rooter, "not me! I was near the pies. I was blowing on them, helping them to cool, until . . ."

"Until what?" asked Mama Rabbit.

"Until a big, fat, dirty pig came along
and pushed me aside and took a carrot pie."

"A dirty pig?" asked Mama Rabbit.

"Oh, yes, a big, fat, dirty, muddy pig," Rooter agreed.

"Oh, my," said Mama Rabbit, "I had better get you into the scrub-up sink!"

Mama Rabbit turned on the hot water, got out the scrub brush, and found the Ironweed soap.

Rooter especially hated the smell
and the sting of that nasty Ironweed soap.
"All set, Rooter, hop in," said Mama.
"Wait a minute," Rooter pleaded. "I just
remembered, it wasn't a dirty pig!"
"Nonsense, Rooter, all pigs are dirty,"
said Mama Rabbit. "Now hop into the sink."
"But it wasn't a pig," said Rooter.

"It was a big dog! He pushed me aside
and took the pot pie," said Rooter.

"A big dog!" exclaimed Mama.

"Uh-huh," said Rooter. "It was that big shaggy dog from down the road."

"Don't move!" warned Mama.

"What's wrong, Mama?"

"That shaggy dog is covered with fleas!"

Mama Rabbit rushed to the medicine chest. "Ah, here is the flea powder!"

"But, Mama—"

"Now, hold still, Rooter, and hold your breath. I'll have to dust you all over."

"Wait!" Rooter shouted. "I forgot, it wasn't a dog!"

"It wasn't?" asked Mama Rabbit.

"No, Mama, it was . . . it was . . . a sneaky fox!"

"A fox!" Mama gasped.
"Heaven help us! Quickly,
children, lock all the doors.
There'll be no picnic today."

"Oh, shucks," said Rhoda.

"But why?" whined Rena.

"What's wrong?" asked
Ricky.

"A fox!" Mama explained.
"A sneaky fox is lurking
around the rabbit hole."

Rooter couldn't look at anyone. He curled himself up in a ball and closed his pink eyes tight. He had never felt so alone in his life. He knew he had ruined everyone's day, and he was truly sorry.

"Mama," said Rooter, as a big, hot tear ran down his face, "I just remembered who ate the pie."

"You mean it wasn't a fox?" asked Mama. Rooter shook his head no.

"Was it the shaggy dog, or the pig?"

"Neither one," said Rooter. "It was me!" he sobbed. "I did it and I'm sorry I spoiled the picnic."

"Well, well," said Mama Rabbit. "I'm sorry that you didn't tell me the truth right away."

"Me, too," said Rooter. "It hurts keeping it inside."

"Well, there's one thing I'm glad about," said Mama Rabbit.

"What's that?" asked Rooter.

"I'm glad there's no fox around!"

Rooter and all the rabbits laughed.

"Can we have our picnic?" asked Rowdy.

"Can we?" asked Rhoda, Rena, Ricky, and Margaret Rose.

"Sure we can," said Mama Rabbit.

So Mama Rabbit and her six bunnies went
down to the meadow. Rooter helped Mama spread
out the picnic cloth. And while Ricky, Rhoda,
Rena, Rowdy, and Margaret Rose ate their carrot
pot pies, Rooter nibbled on clover.

Lies have a way of growing and growing.
They're hard to hide or keep from showing.
Once you start lying, it's hard to stop,
but sooner or later, a lie will pop!